The Dog
Who Changed
the World

The Dog Who Changed The World

Robert Leeson

Illustrated by
Alison Forsythe

Hamish Hamilton
London

HAMISH HAMILTON LTD

Published by the Penguin Group
27 Wrights Lane, London w8 5tz, England
Penguin Books USA Inc., 375 Hudson Street, New York, New York 10014, USA
Penguin Books Australia Ltd, Ringwood, Victoria, Australia
Penguin Books Canada Ltd, 10 Alcorn Avenue, Toronto, Ontario, Canada m4v 3b2
Penguin Books (NZ) Ltd, 182–190 Wairau Road, Auckland 10, New Zealand

Penguin Books Ltd, Registered Offices: Harmondsworth, Middlesex, England

First published in Great Britain 1994 by Hamish Hamilton Ltd

1 3 5 7 9 10 8 6 4 2

British Library Cataloguing in Publication Data
CIP data for this book is available from the British Library

ISBN 0-241-00244-3

Set in 13½pt Palatino by Rowland Phototypesetting Ltd
Bury St Edmunds, Suffolk
Printed in Great Britain by Butler & Tanner Ltd

For Helen and Nicho

First came the bad news. Dad lost his job.

Then came the good news. He found another one.

Then came the bad, bad news.

"It's in a nice little place," Mum gave Sal a funny look. "It's called Yafferton."

Yafferton?

"I don't believe it," said Sal.

Her friends didn't either, but they were very nice about it. They tried not to giggle or stuff their hands in their mouths and shriek and roll on the floor, helpless with laughter. They didn't want to upset her, so they tried hard not to . . .

They were wasting their time. Sal was upset anyway. She was livid. And her brain was working overtime. That night she fixed her mother with a devastating glance.

"We'll have to move, won't we?"

"Ye-es," said Mum. "We were going to tell you. It's – in the country. Dad found this cottage where we can move in right away." She paused. "You'll love it. You remember, last year, we stayed in a cottage."

Sal said nothing. She did remember last year as it happened. The longest week of her life. Up to her eyes in mud, spiders in the washbasin, toilet at the end of the garden, and – yes – those things with claws on her pillow . . .

"A thatched cottage," Mum went on dreamily. "Your bedroom's up under the roof."

Suddenly Sal remembered what those things were called.

"Earwigs!"

Mum stared.

"I'm not coming," Sal went on.

"Oh," Mum eyed her. "What will you do?"

Sal thought on her feet. "I'll stay with Nikki. They've got a bed-settee. I'll get a newsround, or – a milkround. I'll manage."

The worst was that Mum didn't get cross and say, "Don't be silly, you're too young," so that Sal could have a really good row. She just laughed and said, "You? You can't get up on your own."

"I can if I want to. No, I'll stay. You two go."

Dad looked up from the kitchen table where he was filling in forms.

"But we need you, Sal, to look after us in our old age." He smiled winningly at her. "Just come down with the removal van. See if you like it . . ."

"Waste of time," said Sal. "It'll be . . ." she searched around her brain for a word . . . "decrepit."

Mum and Dad fell about the kitchen.

"And it'll be raining," she put in as a clincher.

"Never," said Dad.

But Sal was right.

Sal went to sleep on the journey and woke to hear the rain falling on the removal van roof.

She could see nothing outside but fields and hedges and trees with wet running off them. And some disgusting smell filled the air.

The cottage was just visible through grass and bushes about two metres high.

"Come on," said Dad. "Let's get moving."

They ran to and fro like mad things. Sal's trainers and jeans were soaked.

Later, when they were having a cup of tea and some soggy cake off a box in the little kitchen, Dad said, "This is very handy. You can cook, wash up and lay the table without moving your feet."

He and Mum started to laugh. Sal eyed them with silent contempt.

Mum nudged her. "Look." She pointed out across the muddy back garden full of rampant weeds and rhubarb, like triffids. There was a thick hedge and miles of damp woods beyond. And in front of the hedge was a sort of greenhouse-cum-shed.

"That'll do for my studio," said Mum.

"Well, I could cover the roof and use it as a dark room," put in Dad.

"Hard luck," said Sal. "That's my adventure place. That's where I open the door and vanish into another world and come back years later."

But they were all wrong. The shed got stuffed full with the things they couldn't find room for in the cottage.

"It *is* a bit small," admitted Mum as they all struggled up the narrow, rickety stairs. "Mind your head on those beams, love."

Dad swore. "Too late."

"We'll get used to it," Mum reassured them.

"Hah," sneered Sal.

School was just down the road, just three miles, winding through woods and hedges and ponging farmyards. Dad dropped Sal off on his way to work.

"Have fun," he waved.

Sal ignored that, gripped her lunchbox and marched across the school yard. The locals were staring. She took no notice but she heard one girl say, "Hey, she looks funny."

"Well, she's from down south, isn't she?"

Miss beamed at her, then turned to the class.

"Sally's family has come a long way to

live here. So let's make her welcome."

Thirty pairs of eyes stared at her as though she was something on a slab. One pair of eyes, on either side of a thin red nose, above a tiny mouth, seemed particularly evil. That was the girl who'd been talking in the school yard. Sal knew. Brilliant. Five minutes in the place and she had enemies already.

At lunch break she opened her box and found someone was sharing her sandwiches, someone with eight legs. She fished it out but couldn't help squealing. Just behind her, a girl sniggered.

The day wore on. Mum picked Sal up, smiling nervously at her.

"Was it good, eh?"

Sal didn't even have the strength to make a crushing retort.

Next day was worse. Remarks behind her back, loud enough for her to hear, but not Miss.

No creepy-crawlies in her lunchbox though. No lunchbox. She found it near the end of break under the rubbish hoppers. She felt herself heat up inside. For one moment she felt like marching up to the girl with the nose –

Sharon, she was called – and poking two fingers into those evil eyes. But she had a feeling they'd all gang up on her. She pretended nothing had happened.

She felt like howling, but she didn't. She clenched her teeth till sparks came. Miss tried to help by asking her questions. Sal knew the answers too, even the difficult ones. But instead of being impressed they just made rude noises behind her back. Sharon whispered.

"Talks funny, doesn't she?"

By the end of the week Sal was ready to put her bits and pieces into a handkerchief and run away to sea. Or better still, back home. Home! Real home, the flats, all her friends so close she could pop out on to the balcony and wave or shout to them, school just across the rec., the shops, the club, the swimming pool.

On Friday night she lay in bed, wide-awake. She wasn't listening to the nameless horrors that slid around under the thatch. She'd found out something interesting. The hot water pipe ran up from the kitchen just past the end of her bed. And if she leaned out and listened she could hear Mum and Dad talking down below, when they thought she was asleep.

She lay there hoping to hear Dad say something like, "I can't go on. I'm a failure. Let's go back to civilization."

Or for Mum to say, "I can't stand it here in the sticks, love. I miss the city. Let's go back."

But he didn't and she didn't. Instead, they said, "How's it going?"

"Not bad. The job's OK. Very similar to the old place, though the pace is a bit slower. Decent bunch of blokes. You?"

"Bliss. Lovely views over the woods. Done some watercolours already. Can't think why we didn't move years ago."

Pigs.

There was a silence, then they started talking again but with voices lower. Sal leaned closer to the pipe, till she burnt her nose. But she could just hear.

"Our daughter, though. She's not settling in."

Ah, a bit of sense at last.

"Oh, she will, it just takes time."

Idiots.

"But she *is* lonely."

Now they were starting to notice things. Good.

"Yes, I've been thinking. We ought to do something."

Aha, send her back, eh?

"What have you got in mind?" asked Mum.

Silence for a moment, then Dad said, "There is something she's always wanted, something she was always asking for, but could never have in the flat."

Sal burnt her nose again, but she didn't care; this was getting interesting.

Dad went on, "Something she can have now we're in the country."

She jumped as she heard Mum say, "Aha, I'm with you now. Buy her a dog."

A dog!

Sal bounced up on the bed and shouted.

"A dog!"

There was a sudden silence downstairs. Had they heard her? Then they began talking again. But this time Sal wasn't listening. She was hugging herself, lying in bed and thinking.

Aha, a dog.

CHAPTER 2

Parents can be a real pain. Next day, at breakfast, Sal naturally wanted to get on with the important business of choosing – which dog? She'd been awake half the night making her mind up and narrowed it down to four or five. But down in the kitchen no one said a word about dogs. And she couldn't because she wasn't supposed to be earwigging down the hot water pipes, was she?

So she tried a subtle, roundabout approach.

"I've been thinking . . . " she began.

"Ah, that explains those dark shadows under the eyes," grinned Dad.

Sal ignored him. "It's a bit lonely here in the sticks."

"That doesn't matter, does it? You're not staying, are you?" teased Mum.

Sal was ready for that.

"No," she retorted, "but while I am here, it'd be nice to have intelligent company . . . "

That silenced them.

They looked at her.

"What d'you mean?" they both spoke at once.

"Well, someone you could talk to. Someone who doesn't make sarky remarks when you're trying to be serious."

They looked at each other.

"What d'you mean?" they said, once more.

"Well, like – a pet?"

They were gobsmacked.

"What sort of pet?"

"Oh . . . a St Bernard, say . . . "

"A which?"

"Well, in case one of us got lost in a blizzard on the moors."

They both shook their heads. Whether they were saying "no" or just didn't understand, she couldn't say.

"OK, OK, then, an Irish wolfhound, or a husky, or . . . a Dulux dog."

"Any of those and one of us'd have to move out. This place is too small . . ."

"Tee hee," said Sal.

"Look, be serious," interrupted Mum. "It does so happen, Sal, by a strange coincidence, that your dad and I had sort of thought of buying a dog, but a small one."

"Oh, what a lovely surprise," gasped Sal.

They all three burst out laughing.

In the end the choice was very simple. Dad for once talked sense.

"Let's look at dogs, not pictures in books."

So that weekend they started to drive round to all the kennels they could find – the ones breeding dogs as well as boarding or giving them short back and sides.

In fact they only got as far as one. It lay just off the main road, a couple of miles from Yafferton. At the gateway was a notice, rather like an inn sign, with a painting of two terriers side by side, one black, one white.

"Cor," said Dad. "Just like on the whisky bottle."

"Ooh," said Sal.

"Which one, black or white?" asked Mum.

"Actually – two different breeds," said the lady in charge of the kennels. "The black ones are Scots terriers, the others are West Highland White Terriers."

"Can I see both?" burst out Sal.

The lady shook her head.

"Sorry. Only one litter for sale just now – Westies."

She led them through to the pens. The air was full of dog sounds, whimpers and growls. And every now and then, as if by a signal, the whole pack began to bark deafeningly, then fell silent again.

Four pups huddled on newspapers spread at the foot of their cage, a mass of woolly white, with here and there a triangle of black spots, two eyes and nose. They were like seal babies on the telly, thought Sal. But which one? They seemed so alike.

"I want them all," she said, but no one laughed.

"Can I hold?"

They were taken out of the cage and slowly, carefully, she reached for the first. The black eyes stared at her beneath their white fringes. The coat felt like silk to her touch. Gingerly she began to lift the pup when to her astonishment, it ran over her wrist, scrambled along her arm and had reached her shoulder and was nuzzling her ear before it was rescued.

"Can I have that one?"

"*He's* chosen you," said the kennel lady.

CHAPTER 3

"Six weeks?"

Sal tried to keep her voice down, but she couldn't help it running up into a squeak.

"Sorry, love," said the kennel lady. "But with injections and this and that, it's best for him to stay with us for a while. The time'll soon pass."

She had no idea, thought Sal. That was forty-two days, including six Sundays and they last twice as long – and nights as well. She wouldn't be able to sleep. People had no idea.

Sal marked the day, *The Day*, in red on her

calendar. But it was still on the next page where she couldn't see it. After all, it was unlucky to turn to the next month. So instead she began to cross off each day with a red pencil. But the days didn't go any quicker.

At night she lay awake thinking about the white silk ball with the two black eyes and a black nose and tried to think of names: Rover? No. Flash? No, that sounded like kitchen cleaner. Bonzo? Don't be stupid. Champion? No, that was a horse. How about a Scots name? Hamish? Jock? None of them sounded right. All she could think of was Dog, the Dog.

One day at school, chatting with Miss about this and that, Sal couldn't keep the secret any longer. She blurted it out.

"We're getting a dog . . ."

"That'll make two," whispered Sharon behind her.

The others sniggered. Miss glared at them. Sal wanted to clobber the lot – one by one. But she didn't. There were too many and anyway, she couldn't be bothered.

Instead she went shopping with Mum. They bought:

An eating bowl
A drinking bowl
A round basket bed
A collar
A metal tag, shiny and blank
A lead
A grooming brush
A comb
Powder
Chews you could eat (well, the Dog could)
Chews he couldn't eat
Biscuits

Sal tried one when Mum wasn't looking.

"Yeeuch. It's like iron."

"Good for *him*," said Mum.

Dad had not been idle. He'd borrowed two dog books from the library, and sat in the armchair, reading bits out while Mum and Sal were busy.

"Remember, Sal, he's your dog. You'll have to look after him, even when it's not convenient," he said, then . . .

"Here's an important bit, Sal. He is not, *not*, to sleep in your room."

"Oh, Dad!"

"He'll need feeding three times a day, at first."

"And, don't forget this, Sal. You'll have to let him out at night whenever he needs it. He has to be house trained. It'll take time . . . "

"Yes, lover," said Mum. "Look how long it took with you."

Mum and Sal cleared a space in a corner just inside the front door for Dog's bed and a space in the kitchen by the back door for the feeding bowls.

"The really vital thing," called Dad from the other room, "is for the dog to know his place, to be cared for, but not spoilt, strict discipline, plus affection.

"In the wild, the dog is part of the pack. He always obeys the leader. That's why training is so important."

Dad wandered out into the kitchen where Mum and Sal were sorting out dog things.

"This family will be his new pack. You, Sal, will be like his sister . . . so he won't automatically obey you . . . "

Mum eyed him.

"And who'll be pack leader?"

Dad turned the page.

"It says here the pack is led by the dominant dog, usually male."

"Grrrr," said Mum.

Sal couldn't believe it when at last *The Day* came and they could collect the pup. He'd grown. Now he seemed twice as big, and the coat was coarser where hard hair pushed through the white down on his back.

At first he crouched in the corner, whimpering, ignoring the feeding bowl, even the saucer of milk they put down for him.

"Leave him," said Mum when Sal wanted to pick him up.

In the end they heard the sound of lapping and the chink of the bowl on the kitchen floor.

"We're in business," said Dad.

Sal rushed into the kitchen.

"He's gone," she shouted.

"Can't have, all the doors are shut."

The pack rushed to and fro.

"He's not in the front room."

"He can't have gone upstairs."

No indeed. Dog, refreshed, was busy in the back room.

"Look at that, the little . . . " yelled Dad.

The new pack member, backed up against the bottom bookshelf, was busy puddling some assorted documents.

"Those are my papers!" Dad's voice was shocked.

Sal and Mum fell about.

"Use your authority, pack leader," giggled Mum.

"Grrrrr," said Dad.

Suddenly, after some more mad rushing to and fro, Dog collapsed in exhaustion and was laid to rest in his basket. Sal watched, fascinated by the quick heaving of the little chest. She put a hand on the pup's side and felt the heart beat. He was here, he was alive. She wanted to pick him up and squeeze him, but she resisted the temptation.

The day passed. Dog slept on, woke, drank, ate a bit, made a puddle on the newspapers spread out for him, staggered into his bed and slept again.

It seemed he'd sleep forever. But he did wake at last – when the rest of the pack were fast asleep. From below came the now familiar whining, yipping sound.

"Leave him, Sal!" called Mum as she began to sneak downstairs. "He's got to get used to being on his own."

But the heartrending sound didn't stop, a small miserable whistle, then a yelp, then a treble howl, then a low grizzling whine. It was terrible. Sal couldn't bear it. She decided to make a great sacrifice.

Getting up quietly, she removed Ted from his comfortable place on her pillow and slipped downstairs to tuck the bear in beside Dog. After a while the whining died into snuffles, then small snores. Sal crept back upstairs.

She couldn't sleep; the empty space beside her was very disturbing. Downstairs again. The pup was sleeping soundly. Carefully she manoeuvred Ted's leg from under Dog's head and crept back to her bed.

But barely had she dozed off when she heard that awful yip-yip again. Sighing, she picked up Ted and went downstairs. The pup was half-awake, tottering about, tapering tail flicking to and fro, black eyes on her.

She slid down beside the basket, the pup crawled on to her lap, rump supported by her left wrist, and rested his muzzle on Ted's leg, crooked in her other arm. Slowly the whimpering ceased. Soon they were all asleep.

She woke up in her own bed. Dad was grinning at her.

"What . . . ?" she began. "Where's . . . ?"

"Dog's fine, downstairs, with his new bed partner."

"Ted?"

"Right. Brilliant idea to let him have Ted."

"Oh!" Sal wasn't quite sure.

"Suit yourself, Sal. But listen, tonight leave him be. If he whines, let him. That's an order."

"OK, pack leader," said Sal.

CHAPTER 4

Sal soon discovered that there were two Yaffertons. Upper Yafferton was nearest, about a quarter of a mile from the cottage. It was just one street, well, really a narrow, winding road which climbed over the hill and down to Lower Yafferton. On either side of the road were cottages, a dairy, a little butcher's shop and a post office-cum-general-store-cum-sweet shop.

Then there was Lower Yafferton, which was the big one. That was a laugh, really, but it had streets, a couple of pubs, a church – and the school.

It didn't take Sal long to work out that Dad was driving her to school the long way round. The shorter way was through Upper Yafferton, where the sweet shop was.

And it didn't take much to persuade Dad to drop her off at the top of the hill, so that she could walk down to school on her own.

"The exercise'll do me good," she told Dad.

He stared at her, but said nothing. He was happy to cut down on the chore of driving her the whole way.

But there was a snag to the sweet shop. It was run by Sharon's mother. That was what gave Sharon all the clout at school. In the mornings madame was always behind the counter and Sal could whistle for service. Sharon would always be looking the other way, pretending to be sorting out the stock, or serving her cronies and yakking with them as well.

Sal would wait, slowly simmering, while the clique whispered and giggled and looked sideways at her from the other end of the counter. It was no good making a fuss, she knew; that was just what the Mafia wanted. But she wasn't going to walk out – oh no.

Taking a deep breath she walked, well pushed, past the crowd at the counter, and reached the far end of the shop where a door opened into the kitchen-storeroom at the back.

There, as Sal guessed, sat Sharon's mother, lean and foxy-looking, the image of her daughter, sipping her cup of tea. She eyed Sal suspiciously.

Sal smirked and in her most prissy voice said, "Can I have some chocolate creams? Sorry to bother you, Missus, but your Sharon's busy."

Reluctantly Sharon's mother put down her tea and served Sal without a word, but as Sal left the shop she heard voices raised. Mother and daughter were sorting things out.

Sal discovered something else. As she walked down the hill to school, other kids walked close to her, not right by her, but a little to the front or a little behind.

Then a quiet voice would ask, "What's that dog of yours been up to?"

There was always a lot to tell. Sal would pick special items and dress them up a bit.

"He chews books. He's destroyed a whole shelf full."

Or, "When I get his biscuits out, he does a dance on his hind legs like a circus dog."

Or, "He's not allowed in the kitchen when Mum's cooking so he lies with his nose in the doorway, watching every move. And his nose goes like this . . . "

Dog had stopped whining at night. He slept with his head on Ted's arm. But by day the cottage was full of other sounds – squeals and yowls as someone trod on him.

"Oh Dog!"

"Stupid dog!"

"Oh, poor Dog."

Then Dad had a brainwave – well, he got the idea from the dog book. He dived into the pile of junk in the shed and came beaming back into the house with a battered, brown wooden framework.

"Sal's old playpen."

"You mean, you kept me inside that?" demanded Sal. "It's like a cage. It's a wonder you didn't have the Child Cruelty people round."

"You loved it," claimed Mum, "and so will Dog."

And he did. From his strategic position in

the hall he looked sideways into the front
room, slantways into the back room, forward
into the kitchen and up the stairs, all at the
same time.

He had his chew, his bowl, his Ted, his
newspapers. He lay and watched and slept
and moaned and ate and drank and grew. If
anyone came up the path he would leap in the
air and let out a yipping bark.

"Better than a door bell," said Mum.

Sal told them at school. "We're keeping our
dog in my playpen."

There was a silence. Sal went on hurriedly.
"I don't use it any more."

"You could have fooled me," said Sharon,
loudly.

The class burst out laughing. Sal said
nothing, but slowly smouldered.

CHAPTER 5

"Sal, get up."

Sal blinked, looked round her, her mind muzzy with sleep. It was pitch dark.

"It's not morning," she protested.

"Your dog wants to go out," said Dad.

From downstairs came the familiar whining sound. Sal rubbed her eyes.

"Oh, why?" she moaned.

"Call of nature. Happens to all of us."

"Don't be rotten, Dad. I mean why me?"

"'Cause it's your dog."

"Not every night."

"No, not last night for instance."

"He didn't want to go out last night."

"Oh, he did. Someone else let him out."

"Right," came Mum's voice. "It was me."

Sal struggled up and blundered down the stairs. In the gloom of the hall she saw Dog dancing in his pen, tail flicking. As she bent over the rails he launched himself upwards into her arms and thrust his wet muzzle into her face. She remembered in time to turn away. He settled for a quick lick on her ear, then cascaded out of her grasp, fell half on his head on the carpet and scrambled for the back door.

Sal stood looking out. The night air was chill even if it was May. Outside in the dark she could hear him rustling about.

"Oh, come on, Dog. You've got to have finished," she pleaded.

But lured by a hundred smells in the grass and bushes he padded to and fro.

At last, in desperation, she charged out into the night in her bare feet. Dog heard her coming and shot back into the cottage. When she got back into the hall he was waiting by the playpen. It was only when she was halfway up the stairs that she saw what was on her feet.

"You filthy hound," she screeched.

From above her in the front bedroom she heard quiet chuckling.

"You can laugh, you rotten lot," she shouted.

"You've got to keep at it, love," said Dad. "He's got to be house trained."

Next day was Saturday, fine and warm. Dad cut the back lawn, by hand. The grass was too high for the mower. Sal watched him as he slowly picked up grass clumps with a disgusted look on his face and dropped them into a bin-liner. Suddenly he threw down his rake and swore.

"Filthy – – – – hound."

"Keep at it, love," called Sal. "We've got to get him house trained."

Then quite suddenly, it happened. The playpen was put away and Dog had the run of the house, except the kitchen and the bedrooms.

At night he would move around, sleeping here, sleeping there. Sal could hear his feet clump on the stairs. He was allowed up to the half landing. Or sometimes she could hear him by the patio door, growling at small things creeping along the hedge in the dark.

He was settling down. This was his home. He'd given up attacking the hoover every time the motor started up. And at night he didn't whine to go out. He scratched on the back door. The sound seemed to reach everywhere – and it always woke Sal up.

She took to driving him out into the garden before she went to bed. As he padded back inside she would glare at him and say, "Is that it for the night?"

He would return her glance with just one black eye half hidden by the curving strands of white hair, then amble to his basket.

As he grew his diet changed. Feeding him meat brought its own new excitements.

Sal whispered to her neighbours in class. "Sometimes in the evening, when we're watching television and he's lying half asleep, he farts, very quietly.

"Then Mum looks up and says, 'Out – Dog!'

"And he goes, but he gives her such a dirty look."

The class hooted. Miss looked out of the window. And Sharon, Sal noticed, she wasn't laughing at all.

As the days passed Sal began to feel that she was beginning to get the edge in her daily battle with Sharon. But there was one snag. On her morning walks down the hill to school she had been too successful telling the tale. Now her audience wanted more and more Dog stories.

But more than that they all wanted to see him. Dog was an invisible hero. They knew all about him, but no one had set eyes on him.

Sharon began a whispering campaign. And, being Sharon, she didn't just whisper, either in the yard or in the classroom. She had it to a fine art.

She could talk about Sal without using her name or even looking at her. But she said things Sal knew were meant for her just by lowering her voice when Sal was near.

But it was no good getting annoyed or saying anything.

Sharon would look out of those little eyes and say disdainfully, "Do you mind? This is a private conversation."

But one day, Sharon went too far. She said, quite distinctly, "You don't believe all that rubbish, do you? Has anybody ever seen that dog? She's just making it up."

Sal was just about to make an angry retort, but stopped herself. It was no use swapping insults with Sharon. She had to show Madame. The question was how. First she tried the direct approach with Mum, but got nowhere.

"Can I take Dog to school – please?"

Mum shook her head.

"Can I walk him up to the village?"

"No, love. He's too young yet. Stick to the meadow and the garden. Get him really trained, then, maybe. That's the sensible thing."

Oh, very sensible, thought Sal. But useless. What to do now? Then one day she had an idea.

CHAPTER 6

Dad and Sal were sorting out the shed. Some bits and pieces they stacked against the wall, some they piled on the lawn.

"That can go to the dump," said Dad.

He was quite ruthless, particularly with rubbish belonging to other people in the family.

But Sal stopped him from throwing out one thing, a grey contraption on four wheels.

"Hey, what's that?" she demanded.

He laughed. "Cross between a carry cot and a push chair."

Dad pulled at a lever. "Look, the top lifts

off, so you can carry it by the handles. We used to put you in, tuck you up and wheel you round in it. If we went visiting, we left the wheels outside and lifted you up in the cot part. Look, it's got a hood too. But it's finished. Fall to bits as soon as look."

"Don't chuck it out. Somebody might use it."

"Never. Not posh enough. See those baby carts people have these days – built like Daimlers, or all transparent plastic. No, out on the lawn with it."

"Well, I want it."

Dad stared.

"Get away, Sal." He laughed. "Are you going to wheel Ted round? I thought you'd given up on that sort of thing."

"I might have a use for it." Sal spoke firmly in the way Mum did when she did not want any misunderstanding.

Dad laughed and pushed the contraption back into the shed, then looked round.

"That'll do for now. Let's load up and get off to the dump."

The next stage in Sal's plan needed a little cunning. But it wasn't all that difficult.

"I can walk all the way to school if you like, Dad. It's not that far."

"Are you sure, Sal?"

"Yeah, you can get off in better time for work, can't you?"

"Most considerate." Dad looked a wee bit suspicious.

Sal added hastily, "I can walk with my friends."

That night, as Sal lay in bed, ear close to the hot water pipe, she heard Dad say to Mum, "You know, our daughter's settling in."

"I knew she would," answered Mum. She lowered her voice. "I think Dog helped."

From the hall came a low growl and the pad of footsteps. Mum's voice rose slightly.

"Not you, Dog, we were talking about some other dog. Go to sleep."

Some other dog, thought Sal. There isn't any other Dog.

Sal knew her chance when she saw it. One morning after Dad had driven off, Mum told Sal, "See yourself off today, love. I'm out sketching for a couple of hours."

"What about Dog?" Sal sounded anxious.

"Oh, he's all right for that long. Just you make sure you slam the front door when you go. OK? See you."

"See you," Sal tried to sound casual.

As soon as she heard the garden gate go, Sal went into action. Dog had his eye on her and was at the back door before she reached it.

Just a minute was needed to lug the carriage out of the shed, lift it up the back step and wheel it through the house. The structure wobbled, but it held together. She put in a cushion from the garden seat, and Dog's own blanket.

Already he was dancing on his hind legs, pushing at her with his front paws. She held out her hands, he leapt up. She caught him and laid him on the cushion. For a moment she thought he'd scramble out again, but quickly she spread the blanket over him. Now he lay there, complacently, nose, eyes and ears just visible, one paw sticking out. Sal burst out laughing. Dog looked hurt.

She straightened her face, gave his snout a quick scratch, tucked the blanket in more firmly and pushed the carriage out on to the path, slamming the front door behind her. Outside the lane was empty.

So far so good. Plenty of time, nearly half an hour. She needed to get through Upper Yafferton and down the hill towards school before all the kids were there.

The first doubts came as she reached the road. The wheels squeaked badly and as she began to move uphill, the noise reached screaming pitch. They were nearing the first houses. She looked firmly ahead and tried to be nonchalant, but that awful squealing noise filled the air. Still no kids in sight yet. She pushed on uphill, her heart going thump, thump inside her.

"Good morning, dear."

Sal jumped almost out of her socks. An old woman was leaning over the gate of a cottage.

"Oh, hello."

She felt her cheeks go hot.

"Taking your little brother for a walk?"

Sal swallowed. The old lady began to open the gate.

"Can I see the little love?"

From under the hood came a little warning growl. The woman's eyes opened wider.

"Poor dear. Is his stomach upset?"

"Er, no, he's – er – snoring. I'd better get a move on," Sal said hastily.

She shoved on the handle, prayed that Dog would stay still and quiet. The wheels went up the scale as she quickened her pace.

"'Bye," she called.

"I think you should take him to the doctor. There's something not quite right," the old lady called.

But Sal rushed on.

Now she had reached the shops. Sal didn't dare look though she knew someone was looking out from the sweet shop. They'd seen her. The door opened with a clang. She heard sudden shrieks of laughter. Dog gave another growl.

Sal hurried up the hill. There was more laughter. It followed her over the top of the rise. Squeal went the wheels, grr went the Dog.

"Shh," she told him.

But he growled again and again.

Down the hill was Lower Yafferton. She could see the school now. The yard was empty except for a few early arrivals. Good, she didn't want to meet anyone yet, friend or foe.

"Grrrrr," the growling grew more high-pitched.

But now there was another strange sound. Heavy breathing. She bent over the carriage. That couldn't be Dog, could it?

He growled, then yipped. Then Sal heard another sound – light, running steps. Someone was following her. It couldn't be Sharon and her mates, could it? She quickened her pace, refusing to look round.

Dog stirred restlessly, gave a yap. A car passed. The driver turned at the wheel, stared, grinning, then swerved, straightened up and drove off down the hill.

A sudden awful thought struck Sal. She was being followed, but not by Sharon and Co. Now she did look back.

Behind her were – in this order – a black labrador, a Yorkshire terrier, a spaniel, a poodle and one or two assorted pooches of no pedigree at all. They were coming on purposefully, in single file, breathing heavily as they came. And as they passed the last houses in Upper Yafferton, more dogs appeared, hopping over gates, diving through holes in fences and gaps in hedges.

Sal stopped, stamped her foot.

"Gercha!" she yelled.

The lead labrador stopped, uncertainly. The others bumped into him. Sal pushed on. Dog from his perch growled again. The patter of feet resumed. More cars passed, more stares, more laughter.

A boy on a bike came up the hill, stared, swung wildly and ran up the pavement to crash into the hedge. Sal began to run. So did the dogs.

They reached the foot of the slope and turned into the road that led to school. Looking neither to right nor left, she still knew that there were more people around, on the pavement, getting out of cars; kids, mums, dads, talking, pointing, calling, laughing.

By the school gate a crowd had gathered. The noise grew. Sal made a last effort and came through the school gate with the dogs all around her.

Dog had scrambled up, the hood of the carriage fell back as he placed his front paws on it, head swaying from side to side, teeth bared, growling and snapping at the pack.

The other kids were cheering and waving as Sal rushed across the yard and into the school doorway. From its safety she looked back.

"Are those yours?" The school caretaker was shouting at her.

"N-no," gasped Sal. "Only this one."

Wielding a huge broom he set about the pack, driving it out into the road. Parents joined in and the other dogs fled, knowing they were beaten.

"Well, Sally."

She heard the voice of Miss behind her.

"You'd better bring the dog in. I think we should have a word – before I ring your mother."

The rumpus over Dog died down after a day or two. But that wasn't the end of it.

At home, Sal was in the doghouse. For a whole fortnight, Mum or Dad walked Dog while she fumed at home.

At school Sharon smirked and made remarks behind Sal's back. It was pretty clear that Miss did not want to hear anything from

Sal about her marvellous dog for some time to come.

But other people did. As Sal walked over the hill to school in the morning, or in the school yard during break, the audience for Dog stories grew and grew. Now Class 4 had seen him, they wanted to know more and more. And there was a lot to tell.

CHAPTER 7

Dog went through four hair stages.

When he first came he was soft and silky like a seal pup. Then his outer hair began to grow through the silk and he looked like an arctic fox, ears and snout standing out.

Gradually the soft white undercoat vanished under the shaggy overcoat. He would stand, fore legs firmly apart beneath the deep chest, like a little husky sledge dog.

And last of all he seemed to lose shape altogether, fringes of hair hanging from jaw and flanks, dark eyes almost vanishing in a white mist. Then he looked like a miniature Dulux dog.

The weekly grooming with brush and powder became a struggle as Sal tried to separate the tangles, to rake out the burrs picked up in the meadow, the seeds stuck in his jaw and between his toes.

"Time for his strip," said Mum.

"Strip?"

"Right. That long outer hair has to be pulled out."

"Pulled!" Sal squeaked.

"That's it. If he were a wild dog, the bushes and brambles would comb it out for him. But living indoors, he has to have it done for him."

So off they went to the kennels and left Dog there. When he was picked up again, he was lean and glistening, all the long hair gone save for a ruff round his jaw and under his belly. Ears and tail stood out sharp, bare, slightly pink and very tender. When Sal touched him he growled and snapped. For days he didn't talk to her.

"It's not my fault," she told him.

He clearly didn't believe her. But several sleeps and biscuits later, he seemed to have forgiven her and they were friends again, as if nothing had happened.

Now Sal could get on with Dog's education.

This wasn't as straightforward as she expected for Dog wasn't like other dogs.

He wouldn't sit up and beg. If Sal offered him a biscuit he took it and ate it. Sometimes he took it delicately, sometimes he almost had her hand off.

If Sal threw a ball, he'd look round vaguely as if to say, "Where's that gone?"

Then she'd have to go and get it herself while he followed on behind as though he'd done something smart.

He wouldn't shake hands. He'd sit if you told him (or rather if you asked him nicely) but he wouldn't lie down. In fact he wouldn't do any of the tricks dogs are supposed to do.

Sal worked on him. She trained him every Saturday morning on the big meadow beyond the garden hedge. It was tough going. Dog had definite ideas about why they were in the meadow. The meadow was for sniffing, root-ing in holes and corners and now and then leg-cocking. Or running like mad when something moved just out of reach. He was so busy he hardly had time for her.

But she persisted. And since he was a fair-minded dog and liked her, in the end he agreed to do certain things. He'd come when she called – provided he wasn't too busy right at that moment. If she squatted down, he'd come more quickly.

Getting him to stay when he was running away was harder, but in the end he agreed to do that, when he saw that she was getting just a little bit peeved with him. After a big, big battle, he'd walk to heel (or thereabouts) on the lead.

But that was about her lot. He'd worked out what was important for a happy life and beyond that he wouldn't go. As for performing to order – no. Either he didn't understand or he pretended he didn't.

Slowly Sal realized that Dog had his own view of life. It wasn't self-importance, but it was self-respect.

Sometimes as he moved from tree to tree deciding which one to honour next, he paced like a Lippizaner horse, head up, tail at an angle, raising one paw after another in stately fashion. Sal almost died as she watched.

At the sound of her laughter he turned, stared, head on one side. Then head down he charged at her.

The fact was that Dog had his own tricks. If Sal shone a torch when she let him out in the garden at night, Dog would race madly round and round the flower bed, until he fell exhausted.

If Mum said, "Let's have coffee", or simply, "How about . . . ", he would suddenly appear from whatever corner he had been sleeping in.

When Sal was slow getting his food ready he'd go to the back door and rattle his bowl. If he was told to take his biscuit out of the front room he would lie eating it, nose just a centimetre across the doorway.

If you walked menacingly towards him he would leap from side to side like a bullfighter. Then when you tired of the game, he'd rush forward slyly and nip your ankles.

But best of all, for Sal, the fortnight's house arrest after the great pram fiasco was over. She was taking him out again.

CHAPTER 8

The meadow was full of flowers, the grass full of strange smells and noises. Dog ran to and fro, rooted and yakked, then back home he collapsed, exhausted. In his sleep he twitched and whined and sometimes barked.

"He's a hunter," said Dad, looking up from the dog book. "You know, his breed often follow their prey into small holes in the rocks, get jammed into a cleft and have to stay there for days until they starve enough to slip clear."

"Hey," said Sal. "Like Winnie the Pooh in the rabbit hole."

But he wasn't really much of a hunter. One day on the meadow he started a hare. The orange-brown shape hurtled in giant strides over the grass while Dog ran round barking madly.

Or he would chase the squirrels, who treated it as a huge joke. They would wait until he was almost on top of them, then dodge this way and that, running rings round him. When it seemed he had one, they would leap into the lowest branches of an elder tree, while he yapped hysterically.

Sal would come back from their walks, almost hysterical too – with laughter.

"I had a real job keeping him out of the wood, you know," she told Mum. "He's dying to get in there."

"Well, he can die," said Mum severely. "He's not going and neither are you. That'll have to wait."

"Oh, Mum. You are a pain. It looks great in the woods. There's a stream and everything."

"I know. That's just what I mean. For now, you keep him in the meadow. He can't come to harm there."

Famous last words.

One evening as Sal and Dog breezed into the house, Dad looked up and sniffed.

"Good grief, what a pong."

Sal giggled. "I couldn't stop him. You know at the end of the field where the cows stand when they wait for milking? He found a lovely patch and rolled in it."

"Take him outside and clean him up. He smells foul. You don't smell much better either. Check your shoes."

"Thank you," retorted Sal.

Then as she drove Dog out into the garden she looked back.

"I bet there aren't any cow pats in the woods."

"Don't be cheeky."

But Dog found more than cow pats in the meadow.

One morning he spotted a movement by the high hedge. Ignoring Sal's call, he charged off, barking madly.

A few seconds later he came back, even faster, tail between his legs. Behind his fleeing figure, through the screen of long grass and nettles, came an awesome sight.

It was large, mottled red and grey, fur standing on end like spikes, wicked green eyes sparkling. Sal felt her stomach go cold. What was it?

She grabbed a stick from the ground and advanced more boldly than she felt. Dog advanced boldly, too, but a metre behind her.

At the last moment the green-eyed monster stared contemptuously at Sal, flicked its tail and turned away to vanish through the hedge.

At school that day she gave her audience a graphic account of how Dog, with her help, had fought off this wild beast – a pine marten or a pole cat or something. She described it in detail down to the evil green eyes. It was a great performance and they listened wide-eyed.

The only snag was Sharon. She seemed to think it was funny. But she said nothing.

"Your daughter's in trouble again."

Lying in bed that night, Sal could hear Dad's voice from the kitchen.

It was funny, she thought. When there was something good, Mum and Dad always said "our daughter". When it was trouble it was "your daughter".

"What's she been up to now?"

"While you were out I had a visit from Mrs Burgess. She has the next cottage down the lane. First time I've spoken to her."

"Oh, that was nice."

"No, it wasn't. She's terrifying. Lean and hungry-looking. She walks with a stick, but I don't think she needs it for support. She kept waving it in the air."

"What was wrong?"

"It seems that Dog, aided by Sal, armed with a stick, terrorized her poor little cat. They chased it through the hedge into her garden. The poor thing was so alarmed it hid under the stairs and wouldn't come out."

Sal felt a sudden rush of indignation. She was almost ready to rush downstairs and protest, when she remembered she was not supposed to know what they were saying. Mum went on.

"What did you say to Mrs Burgess?"

"What could I say? I grovelled. I told her I'd put them both on bread and water for a week."

There was silence. Sal felt herself coming to the boil. It wasn't that she believed the bit about bread and water – well, not much. But the unfairness of it.

Getting caught out when you've done something is bad. Getting flak when you've done nothing was – too much. But she calmed down a little when she heard Mum say, "I'm not sure you know how to deal with the village ladies. Next time, leave them to me."

"If you say so. But what shall we do?"

"Well, first I'll go round and see how Poor Pussy is. Then we'll have to see what to do about Dog."

Chapter 9

"On the lead! All the time?"

Sal looked across the breakfast table at Mum. She tried to sound surprised, which was difficult. But she had no problem sounding indignant. She was choked.

"Sorry, love."

"But I didn't touch her rotten cat. I didn't even know it was a cat. It looked too big. That's why I grabbed a stick. And Dog was scared stiff."

Dog looked up from the corner, ears drooping, eyes full of concern.

"Ha, ha," said Mum. She looked at Sal.

61

"You know, love, Dog is going to get a bad reputation. You know what it's like in a village – give a dog a bad name."

Dog's ears drooped even more. Sal nodded. Yes, she did know what it was like in a village. Or she was beginning to find out.

"So. Keep him on the lead and you can't go wrong."

Famous last words.

Life was quiet for a few days at home and at school. Once or twice Sal saw Mrs Burgess, tall, grey-haired, erect as a soldier, standing at her gate, glaring out at the world. She wondered if she should go up to her and apologize. But then she thought – no, Dog's done nothing wrong. I've done nothing wrong. And nothing happened with that horrible cat of hers.

So Sal kept to the other side of the road, looked down and walked demurely on up the hill to Upper Yafferton.

And twice a day, morning and evening, Sal and Dog, handcuffed together, walked sedately round the meadow like an old married couple!

Now that Dog wasn't allowed to run on his own she had to give him a longer walk on his lead, for the sake of exercise. That meant changing her habits – getting up earlier.

This was hard enough – the getting up part. But worse was to come, and quickly.

On the first "early" morning they made their erratic way along the edge of the meadow, where it ran side by side with the deep, green, enticing wood.

Dog was very frisky, darting here and there, rushing ahead, stopping, pulling back, irritatingly spending hours over one particular tree root before raising his hind leg to bless it.

Sal got bored. She looked around while he messed about. But her mind was busy. How was she going to crack this problem of Dog and this totally unfair accusation of cat mugging?

It was hard enough on Dog, but she couldn't spend the rest of her life tied to this hound, much as she loved him. How to clear his name?

She brooded, looked up at the sky, yawned and automatically tugged on his lead, saying, "Oh, come on Dog, I'll be late for school."

So Sal was totally unprepared for what happened next.

There was a crashing of bushes, a deep bark, a howl of terror from Dog. A huge shadow brushed past her. The lead jerked in her hands as he tried to snatch himself free.

But the leather was caught on her wrist. Another woof, a whimper and Dog was twisting madly round and round her ankles. Trying to catch hold of him, she tripped, stumbled and fell backwards into the long grass, with Dog half under her.

She stared upwards and to her horror the sky seemed to be blocked out by a great hairy snout, pointed ears and deep dark eyes, which bent over her. The muzzle was flecked with spittle. Sal screamed.

"Mack, Mack! Heel, heel!"

Sal heard the boy's voice, shrill with alarm, behind her. There was more rustling in the hedge. Then the big dog's face moved away.

Dog and Sal struggled up. She unwound the lead, stroking the white, quivering head. Her fear vanished. Now she was angry.

"You stupid idiot!" she yelled. "Can't you control your stupid animal?"

Then she stopped and stared.

The alsatian, perfectly still, sat on its haunches two metres away, panting gently. By its side, and not all that much taller, but with a firm hand on its collar, was a boy.

He was thin and pale with large spectacles. Their thick lenses magnified the blue eyes under his light brown hair.

"Oh, it's you," was all she could say.

It was Andy, one of the group who listened to her Dog stories in the morning. He was smaller than her, younger too, and very, very shy.

Once or twice it had seemed he'd been about to speak but when she'd looked at him he'd turned red and looked away. He was blushing now.

"I'm sorry," he said at last. "Mack wouldn't hurt anybody. He scented your dog and rushed through the hedge before I knew, like. He just wanted to play. And I wasn't expecting you to be here. I mean, normally there's nobody around at this time – honest."

After this long speech he fell silent. Sal was silent too, but her mind was working fast. She looked down. Dog had recovered his spirits.

His snout and ears pointed up again as he faced the other dog.

A silent communication was taking place. Then Dog's tail began to wag. Big Mack's tail began to move slowly from side to side. He rose under Andy's gaze but did not move forward. Dog trotted to the end of his lead and their noses touched.

Andy looked at Sal.

"See, friends."

She let her breath go, but she kept her voice prim.

"If you're sure."

"'Course I'm sure. Hey, are you coming out at this time tomorrow? . . . I mean . . . " Now he was turning red again.

A smile spread across Sal's face.

"Tell you what, Andy. Will you do me a favour?"

"What?" he asked eagerly.

"Come and talk to my mum."

CHAPTER 10

Mum was quite taken with the small boy in glasses and even more with the alsatian with the massive head and large, watchful eyes.

"I suppose it'll be OK, Sal. I'm sure Andy and Mack know their way around. Just make sure you and Dog don't do anything that they wouldn't do. But only off the lead in the woods, mind."

So, that evening, the four took their first walk together in the woods. It was great, it was exciting. It was very nearly a disaster.

The wood was a maze of paths, running here and there under great oaks and beeches and chestnut trees, among bushes and clumps of fern. Through it all ran a stream, sometimes narrow and rushing between high banks, sometimes broad and shallow.

Off the lead now, Dog went wild, racing crazily up and down, rolling in the wild garlic, mock-fighting with the amiable Mack, who could have eaten him at one gulp but who seemed to enjoy letting the smaller animal rag him.

Sal and Andy wandered along talking about school. She discovered that he too had been tormented by Sharon and the Mafia. He looked at her.

"It's 'cause we're incomers," he explained.

"Incomers?"

"Yeah, you know, new people. From outside. Not born here."

"But we've been here ages," protested Sal.

"Not born here though," said Andy.

While they talked, the dogs appeared and disappeared, barking, panting, leaping up to greet them, then dashing away again. But no matter how excitable the chase, a call from the boy would bring Mack back with Dog close behind.

That was until Dog discovered water. Mack played a fine game, charging at full speed to the stream, then taking off in a full-stretch leap to land on the farther side.

Without hesitation Dog followed like a white streak, launching into the air to land flat in the middle of the brook.

Sal rushed to the bank. "Quick, get him out. He can't swim. He'll drown."

But he could and he didn't. Instead of being rescued he paddled around, splashing and snorting. Mack leapt in beside him. Only with a great deal of coaxing were they brought out of the water, to stand spraying most of it over Sal and Andy.

They reached Sal's home just before it got dark. Mum stared at the two of them, then at the dogs, both of whom were covered in a coat of green weed and slime.

"Oh, Andy," she said reproachfully. "I thought I could trust you to keep them out of trouble."

Andy looked down, red-faced. Sal giggled.

"You've got it the wrong way round, Mum. Dog found the pond first. Mack went in after him."

Mum grinned. "OK. I believe you. Would you like to stay for supper, Andy?"

Things should have settled down now, but as it happened, they came to a head, and very quickly.

Every morning and evening Sal and Andy walked the dogs – in the meadow or through the woods. Mrs Burgess's cat kept out of sight.

But someone else had their eye on them. After the morning dog-walk, Sal and Andy set off to school together. They had so much to talk about that they didn't notice anything or anybody else, till they were in the school yard.

Then they heard the familiar sneering voice.

"Oh look, she's got herself a toy boy."

Sal looked up to see Sharon and her cronies right in front of them. There was no way they could get into school without pushing right through them.

"Look at him. He's blushing," went on Sharon derisively. She nudged her nearest friend. "What d'you reckon they were doing in Barker's Wood last night – walking the dog, eh? That's what they call it."

The sniggering burst into open laughter. Sal

glanced sideways at Andy. He looked as though he wanted to run home.

But suddenly Sal felt a surge of joy. This, she realized, was the moment she'd been waiting for. While Andy looked on in horror, she marched forward until she was centimetres away from Sharon. The foxy little eyes were uncertain now. Sal raised her hand.

But instead of hitting Sharon, she reached out slowly and taking that sharp nose between her fingers, she twisted it.

"Excuse me," she said with great deliberation. "Do you mind if my friend and I come past?"

Sharon did not say a word, or utter a sound. Her heart was too full. Eyes watering, she backed away while Andy and Sal marched across the silent playground into school.

That evening Dad looked out of the front window. He turned to Mum.

"Remember what you said about dealing with the village ladies, love?"

"Yes?" said Mum, curiously.

"Well, now's your chance. Mrs Whatsit

from the sweet shop's coming up the path. She looks as though she's got something on her mind."

CHAPTER 11

Saturday was gorgeous, warm and sunny. Sal and Andy took the dogs for a long, long walk, beyond the woods, down the winding lanes, where Sal had never been. She had little to say and Andy looked at her anxiously.

"What's up?"

She shrugged. "Oh, nothing."

"Doesn't look like nothing."

"Oh well . . . " She told him about Sharon's mother coming to the house, all the complaints, and the threats. Sal imitated the voice.

"This could be a prosecution matter. It was a vicious assault."

Andy's eyes opened wider.

"You mean, Sharon's nose?"

"Right."

"What did your mum and dad do?"

Sal frowned at the question.

"That's the worst thing. They wanted me to apologize to Sharon."

"Get off. They didn't?"

"Well, they reckoned I'd no business – attacking her."

"But you didn't attack her. I mean, you just, like, pulled her nose. And after what she's done . . . " He looked at Sal. "Sharon's mother doesn't say, 'Sharon, have you been annoying people?' She says, 'Who's been bullying my lovely little girl?' Honest . . . " He broke off in disgust.

This made Sal laugh. Andy was more choked than she was.

"Andy, why's Sharon down on me? What have I done?"

He shook his head. "Nothing, Sal. She just wants to rule the roost at school, like her mother does in Upper Yafferton. Whenever somebody new comes, she starts on them, talking behind their backs, playing tricks. If you answer her back, she shouts you down. If you try to get even, she puts you in the wrong."

He made a face. "I hate rows. So I just try to keep out of her way and hope she'll leave me alone."

Sal nodded.

"Thing is," went on Andy, "it didn't work with you. You're not afraid of her."

"It's funny," mused Sal, "but she's got worse since I got him." She pointed at Dog, who stopped where he was rooting in the grass verge and looked inquiringly at her.

Andy laughed. "I expect she's jealous."

Sal bent to scratch Dog's head.

"Who wouldn't be? I mean, he is fantastic. There isn't a dog anywhere anything like him." She stopped. "I'm sorry, Andy. I mean like him and Mack."

He grinned, then beckoned the alsatian who trotted up. Andy clipped on the broad leather lead.

"What's up?" she asked.

He nodded towards a bend in the narrow lane.

"Two farms down there."

"Oh, he wouldn't attack anything, not Mack."

"No-o," said Andy slowly. "But once when he was very young, he ran into one of these farms. He wanted – to play with the hens. I managed to catch him, but the farmer ran out and said he'd shoot him if he came in again."

"That's rotten."

"Can't blame him, Sal."

Sal shrugged. "Oh, well."

She snapped Dog's lead on. They rounded the bend and the farm buildings came into view.

"What a pong!"

The effect on Dog was dramatic. He began to pull at his lead – no, jerk – fiercely. At the farm entrance he ran forward, then leaped aside, dodged behind Sal and began to haul backwards with all his might.

"Knock it off, Dog," snapped Sal.

"What's up with him?" asked Andy.

"I've no idea. But if he doesn't stop . . . " Sal gave a warning tug on the lead.

"Heel!" she commanded.

Reluctantly Dog did as he was told. They walked on, leaving the farm behind, but for nearly half a mile Dog hung back, having to be dragged along. He did not stop until they reached the woods. Andy let Mack go and the big dog rushed away. Dog followed. Barking sounded through the trees.

Sal and Andy wandered along. They raced sticks in the stream, jumped over the water with the dogs, then sat on a log, chatting of this and that. Towards tea time they came out on to the meadow and Andy turned to go home.

"See you tomorrow, Sal."

"You bet."

She caught Dog, clipped on his lead. She noticed the collar was frayed, where he had been pulling. She'd have to fix that when she got home or buy another.

She waved to Andy and walked over to the lane. It was funny; usually near home Dog would rush ahead, but now he was trailing behind as though he were tired. Idly she let her arm swing back behind her, keeping a firm grasp on the loop of the lead, but letting him make his own pace.

She leaned on the gate thinking about the day. And her mind went back to Sharon. But now she didn't feel bothered any more. It was all too ridiculous. There was Andy and her, Mack and Dog. What did anybody else matter?

She reached out to open the gate.

"Come on, Dog. Tea time."

There was no sound. She pulled on the lead. It was loose. Now she looked down.

There was no – Dog.

The long meadow, reaching out to the woods, was empty. The worn collar, snapped across, hung at the end of the strap.

CHAPTER 12

Mum and Dad looked up in alarm as Sal, pale-faced, holding the broken collar, ran into the kitchen.

"Dog's gone."

"He can't have," they both said at once.

But they got to their feet.

"We came back through the woods. He was on the lead right across the meadow. I just stopped by the gate for a minute . . . then I looked down and . . . "

"That collar ought to have been fixed," said Dad severely.

"Oh, I know," shouted Sal. "What's the use . . ."

Mum intervened.

"Look, love. Give Andy a call. He'll help you look. Dog's bound to be in the woods. Mack'll find him. He must have sneaked back to roll in that green pond."

"That's it," said Sal eagerly, running to the phone.

Dad turned to the back door.

"I'll get the car out and look down the lanes," he said. He looked at Mum. "Will you hang on here in case he wanders back?"

Andy, Sal and Mack searched the woods from end to end and Mack wandered fretfully round the edges. But there was no Dog. They explored the bushes, the stream, the pond, and the bank where the rabbits had their warren. But there was neither sight nor sound.

"Better go back. It's getting dark." Andy put his hand on Sal's shoulder. "He'll be somewhere. He's probably got into someone's garden and can't find his way out."

Sal didn't want to go.

"Suppose he's down one of those rabbit holes – stuck."

"No, Sal. If he'd spotted a rabbit they'd have heard the racket over in Yafferton, honest. I don't think he's here. He must have run home. Come on."

Sal ran home, breathless, her chest hurting. But there was no Dog. Dad and Mum looked at her anxiously.

"I've rung the police," Dad said. "They told me they'd keep an eye open for him."

"What's the good of that?" snapped Sal.

"Love, I expect they've got . . . " Mum hesitated, " . . . lots of other things to do."

What other things? What could be more important than finding Dog?

"Anything could happen to him . . . he . . ."

Sal stopped. She did not really want to list the things that could happen to Dog.

That night she dreamed, an awful dream. She was struggling through dark, dank tunnels. She was calling and she could hear Dog barking. But the more she looked, the fainter the sound became. She woke to hear Mum's voice.

"Andy's here, love."

Boy and dog waited on the garden path and without a word all three went to comb the woods again. They looked behind every bush, under every overhang by the stream. But there was no Dog.

The rest of Sunday passed slowly. The phone rang twice, but not with news of Dog. In the evening Andy came again and quietly offered Sal Mack's lead.

But she shook her head.

"Sorry, Andy. Don't want to come out."

"OK. See you tomorrow."

She went back to her room. The evening went. Dark came. She slept and dreamt and woke, then slept again.

By the time she got to school on Monday, word seemed to have got round. Everyone knew. But this was one morning when for once she did not want to talk about Dog.

Some kids offered advice, where she should look, who she should tell. Some told her stories about dogs who had been missing for – oh – months, then turned up from hundreds of miles away.

Sharon stood to one side with her clique, whispering.

"Probably got run over. I mean anybody with any sense'd look after it, wouldn't they?"

Sal just pretended she had not heard. She waited for school to end, then ran all the way home.

Mum met her in the doorway and Sal knew that there was no news.

"People have promised to look out for him. But . . . I'm afraid . . ."

But Sal did not want to know what Mum was afraid about. She had a sudden thought.

"We could put a notice in the shop."

Mum's lips pursed thoughtfully.

"Are you sure, Sal? I could do it for you."

Sal knew what she meant, but said stubbornly, "No, I'll do it, now."

She walked slowly up the hill to the shop, working out, as she went, what she would say. She'd begin by telling Sharon that she was sorry about the nose job. It would choke her, but she'd do it. Then she'd say, casually, "I'd like to put this notice in the window, please."

But it didn't work like that. Sharon's foxy little eyes spotted the card and the fifty pence coin in Sal's hand and she said, in a studied, casual way, "The board's full. Why not bring it back on Friday, when some cards'll be coming out?"

"Friday!" Sal's voice was shrill.

There was a clang from the shop doorbell. Someone had come in behind her.

"It's urgent," she went on more quietly. "I've got to try and find my dog." She swallowed. "Look, Sharon. I know you don't like me. I'm sorry we had that fight. But my dog . . ."

Sharon's smirk became broader. Her voice became more prissy and affected.

"I'm sorry, it's just not possible."

Sal felt a flush of rage. Trying to keep her voice down, with other people listening, made the words come out in a strangled way.

"Sharon. You've got no right. It's my dog."

Sharon's voice rose. Sal knew this was for the benefit of her mother sitting in the back room with her cup of tea.

"We are not forced to accept any notice. This is just a service."

Sal felt the tears sting behind her eyelids. She was beaten. But she wouldn't let Sharon see. She turned and rushed from the shop.

The woman in the doorway, leaning on her stick, tried to move aside, but Sal bumped into her. It was Mrs Burgess.

Shouting a hasty "Sorry", Sal flung open the door and blundered into the street. Her heart thumped and blood pounded in her ears. Vaguely she heard Mrs Burgess's rasping voice.

"Just a minute, young woman."

But Sal did not stop. She ran on, back down the slope, into the lane, up the garden path and into the kitchen again.

Mum looked at her flushed face, then came round the table to put her arm round Sal's shoulders.

"Love, I know it's hard. But you may have to face the fact. Dog may have – gone. Listen, we'll get another . . . "

Another? Another. There wasn't another – anywhere.

CHAPTER 13

T hat evening, Sal and Andy walked across the meadow, Sal holding Mack's lead. The big dog walked at her heel, tail down.

"Want to have another look in the woods?"

Sal shook her head.

"D'you think he's gone, Andy?"

"No, Sal. He'll turn up," said Andy.

But he didn't sound as though he really believed it.

Sal told him about what had happened in the shop, then added, "If Sharon says a word tomorrow, I'll destroy her."

Andy's mouth fell open as he saw her

expression. Then he cleared his throat.

"Yeah, you do just that."

As they parted at the end of the lane, he said, "Any time you want to take Mack out, just give me a call."

"Thanks, Andy."

"See you."

"See you."

Wandering home she half saw the big mud-stained Range Rover in the road. And she half saw the man in shirt-sleeves, breeches and boots. But she clearly saw Mrs Burgess leaning on her stick and pointing.

"That's her."

The sharp voice reached Sal. What did the old woman want? She'd said sorry when she'd bumped into her in the shop, hadn't she? And who was this man?

He stepped forward, face serious.

"Are you Sally Foster?"

"Ye-es. I live here." She pointed at the cottage, then tried to pass him but he did not make way. Instead he turned and picked something up from the bonnet of the vehicle. It was like a fruit hamper. He held it crooked in one arm.

Then looking keenly at her he said, "Do you recognize . . . ?"

The lid went back. Deep in the wicker frame was a still bundle of white hair. Sal's stomach went cold. She couldn't speak. Her chest had tightened till it hurt.

Then there was an explosion from the basket. Something moist hit her face and claws scrabbled at her clothes.

"Oh," she gasped.

"He's yours all right, girl," said the man.

She pulled Dog away from her face and stared. The man's brown, wrinkled face was smiling now. But he looked somehow embarrassed.

"Where did you find him?" Her voice came out as a squeak.

"I didn't. He found us."

"I don't know what you mean," gasped Sal.

Then she stopped as she heard frantic barking from the Range Rover. Dancing up and down, pawing the windscreen, was – Dog. No, it couldn't be. He was squirming in her arms.

The man grinned.

"Our Mag. We call her Mag 'cause she

scolds like a magpie." He paused. "Your dog came to our farm Saturday evening, out of the blue." He pointed away towards the woods.

Now Sal remembered.

"Right. We were passing a farm and he went berserk. I had no end of trouble getting him away. He went all the way back!"

"That's him. He scented our Mag, and he sneaked back. That breed's very cunning. I didn't know what to do. No collar, see."

He stopped. "I hope you didn't think I was keeping him."

Sal burst out, "Andy said you'd once threatened to shoot his dog."

He frowned as if remembering, then smiled ruefully.

"Still, he *was* among the livestock. But I love dogs, Sally, believe me. If I'd known who owned this chap I'd have brought him back there and then."

"But how did you find out?"

"Mrs Burgess phoned."

Sal stared, baffled. Then she looked beyond the man. They were alone now. Mrs Burgess seemed to have gone.

"But how could she know?" she asked.

"She didn't, love. What she did was ring round all the farms this afternoon on the off-chance."

He grinned apologetically.

"She's a – funny old lady. But she's very shrewd."

"But I thought she hated dogs."

"I expect she does. But she told me she didn't like to see anyone upset over their pet."

"So she kept on ringing."

He smiled at her. "People round here are like that, you know. Like to help each other, if they can."

As the farmer drove away, with Mag frantically barking from the front, Sal walked back up the garden path, hugging Dog to her. The front door burst open. Mum and Dad were there, grinning at her. Dog tumbled out of her arms and leapt up the step, pawing them and barking his head off.

Then Sal stopped on the path and turned round.

"Hey, where are you off to?" said Dad.

"I've got to go round and tell Andy."

She ran down the road. But she wasn't just thinking about Andy. She was thinking about tomorrow. She couldn't wait to get to school and tell them all.

Dog was back and everything in the world was fine.

One of the best books about Westies is
The Complete Illustrated West Highland White Terrier,
edited by Joe and Liz Cartledge
(Ebury Press, 1973)
which can be found in libraries.